D0770940

BOO TO YOU, WINNIE THE POOH!

 Adapted by Bruce Talkington

Illustrated by Robbin Cuddy

NEW YORK

 For information address Disney Press, 114 Fifth Avenue, New York, New York, 10011-5690.
Printed in the United States of America.

Library of Congress Catalog Card Number: 96-84274
ISBN:0-7868-3151-0

First Edition
5 7 9 10 8 6 4

Based upon the animated special *Boo! To You Too! Winnie the Pooh*
written by Carter Crocker, directed by Rob LaDuca.

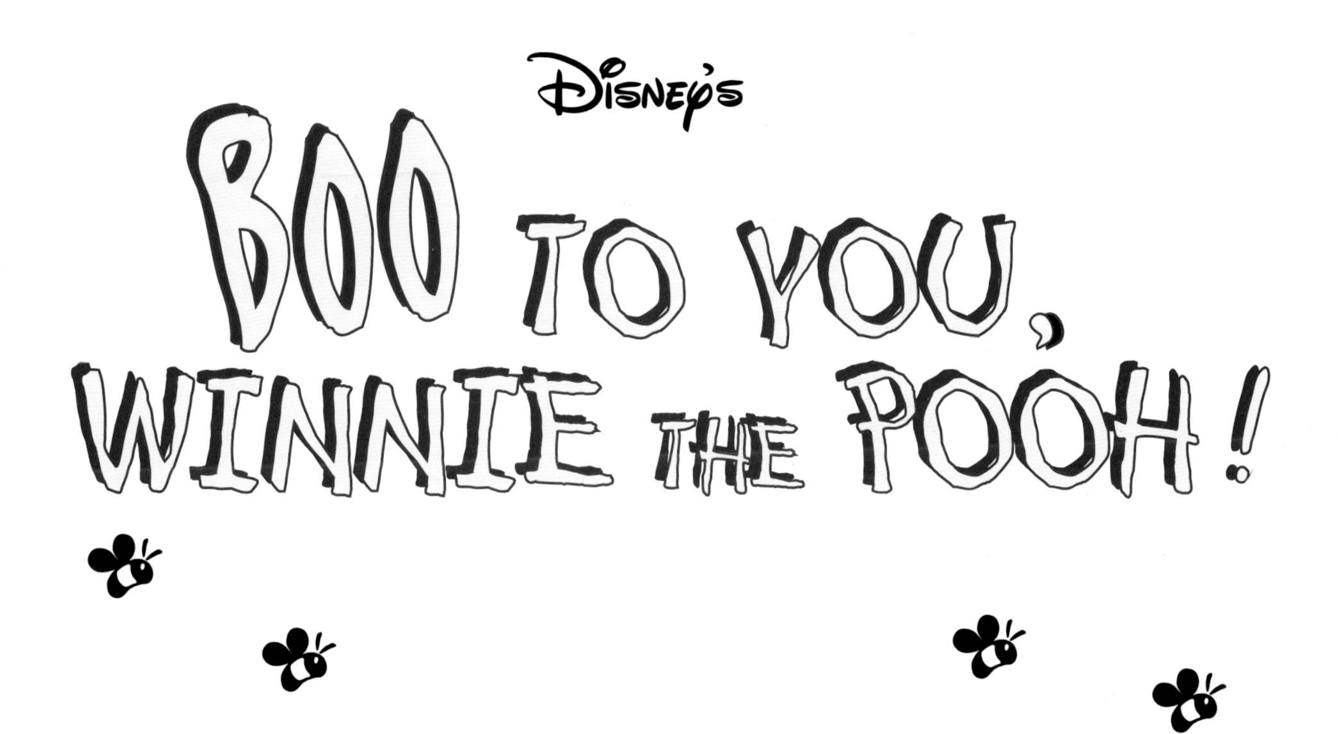
Disney's
BOO TO YOU,
WINNIE THE POOH!

HUNNY

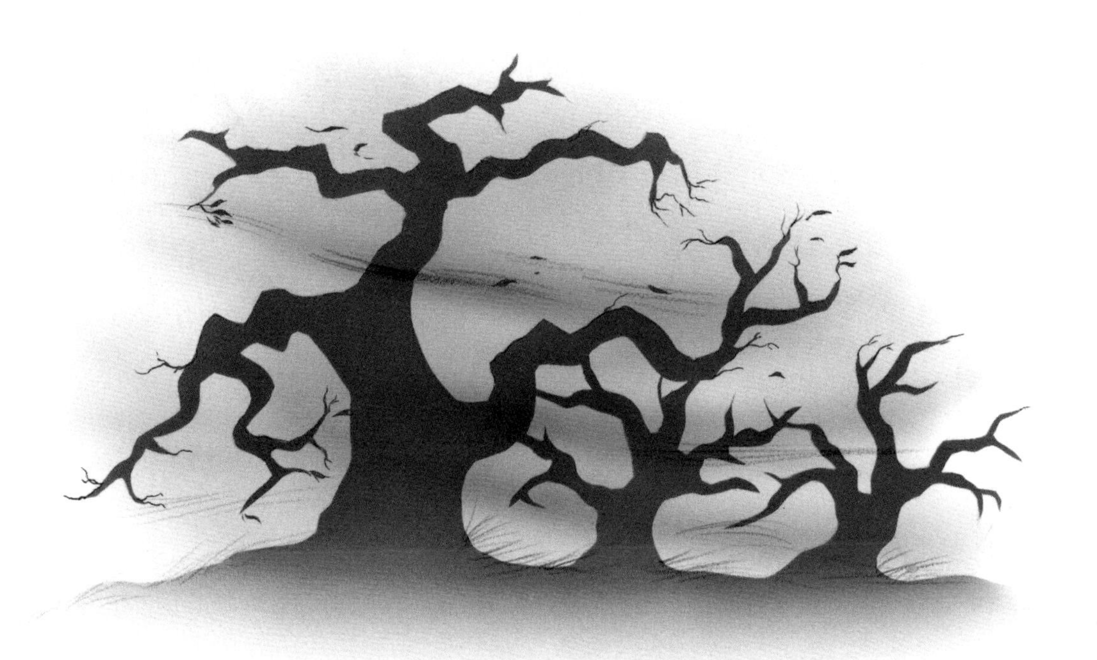

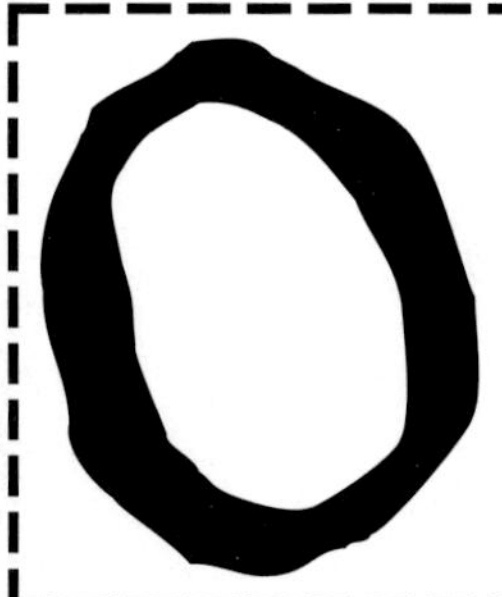

nce each year, as October breezes puff and bluster, there comes a most particular and most peculiar night, when the dark grows a little more so, and the trees jitter and rattle their leaves until they chatter like frightened teeth. And on this particular and peculiar night at the house of Winnie the Pooh, the bear was seated in the middle of his floor, dressed as a giant bee and pouring the contents of a large crock of honey into his mouth.

"Practicing for Halloween," he chuckled between gulps. "Though I'm not fond of tricking, I do enjoy the treating . . . especially of myself."

Just as Pooh was savoring the last small smackeral of sweetness, a creature in baggy pajamas with a skeleton painted on them bounced Pooh, and the two of them went rolling across the floor in a tangle.

"Not late, am I, buddy boy?" hooted Tigger, for, of course, that is who the bouncer was. "Halloween's what Tiggers and skeletons do best, 'cause nothin's more fundamental than *fun*! Hoo-hoo-*hoo*!"

Behind the delighted feline were *two* Eeyores, one wrapped in bandages like a mummy and the other a sort of bedraggled Eeyore-like creature.

"See? Even donkey boy's precipitatin'!" Tigger pointed out.

"Hello, Eeyore," said Pooh to the mummified donkey. "And hello, Gopher," he chuckled to the other Eeyore.

"Ding dagnabbit!" snapped Gopher ruefully. "How am I supposed to win the best-costume contest if you know it's *me*?!" Gopher stomped off, muttering to himself. "I'll surprise 'em yet! Just wait and see!"

"Best-costume contest!" exclaimed Tigger. "C'mon, Poohster! We better get a move on!"

"Not," Pooh said with surprising determination for such an easy-going bear, "until our good friend Piglet can join us."

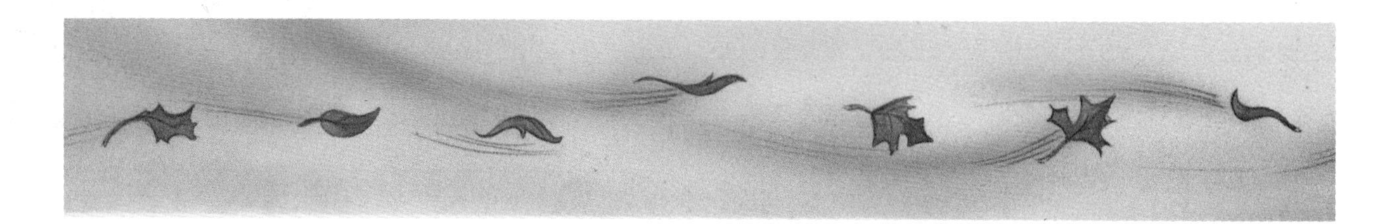

And while they were making plans to include their very small friend, strange happenings were happening at Piglet's house as he made his own preparations for Halloween. Crouched in the middle of his parlor was the most horrible pretend spookable that the very small animal could put together, a monstrosity of household gadgets, fabric, and chair legs topped with a leaky colander (as if there were any other kind) for its head.

"If I'm not scared of something as fright-*full* as this," Piglet told himself, "I won't be afraid of anything this Halloween."

At that moment, the front door was flung open and Piglet was joyfully bounced by Tigger the skeleton.

"Boo-hoo-*hoo*!" shouted the bone-bedecked feline.

"Why, Piglet," exclaimed the surprised Pooh, "where's your costume?"

"Yeah, lookit the time, Pigletto!" said Tigger, pointing out the window. "It's half past a quarter to sunset!" He began leading Piglet toward the door. "We gotta get to Halloweenin'!"

"Oh . . . uh . . . I . . . ," Piglet stammered, searching for a suitable explanation.

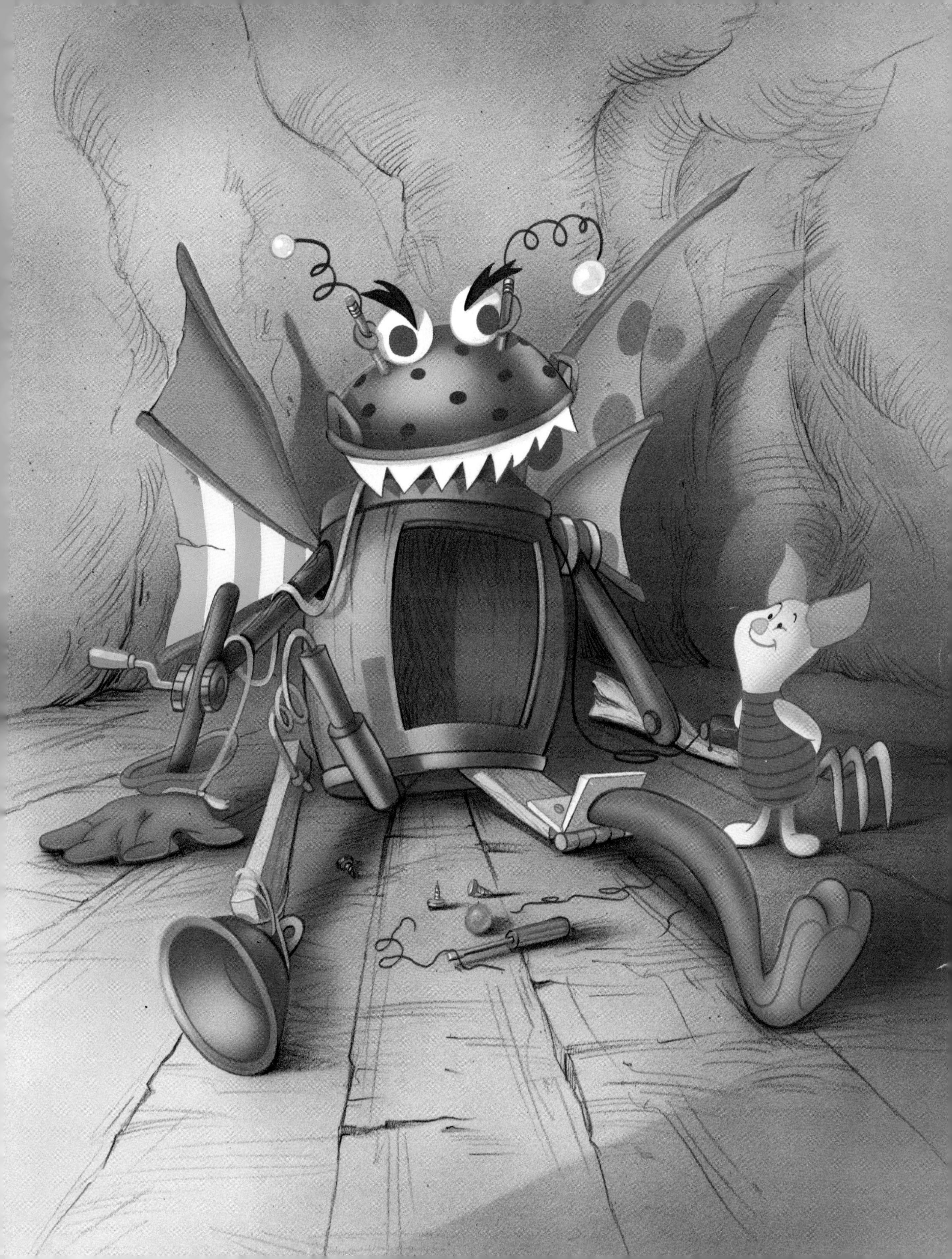

“And while Piglet is figuring out what he will be this Halloween,” announced Pooh, “I think I should try out my costume by being all the bee I can be and tricking a small smackeral of something sweet from our friends at the honey tree.”

“But, Pooh—,” Piglet began to protest.

“Perhaps it would be best, Piglet,” interrupted Pooh, “if you didn’t call me by my given name.” And he whispered to Piglet as an afterthought. “It might make the bees suspicious.”

"Enough jabberin'," hooted Tigger. "Let's get to terrifryin'!"

So, much to little Piglet's distress, they all followed Pooh off to trick-or-treat the honeybees.

But they were on their way back almost immediately (if not sooner), running as fast as they could with a blizzard of angrily buzzing bees close behind!

"Oh dear!" gasped Pooh between pants, "I'm not the bee I used to be."

Not too far down the path, Rabbit was in the midst of his pumpkin patch, chest swelling with pride as he stepped from one pumpkin to another, giving each a pat, a polishing, or a fussy rearrangement of a vine.

"Ahhh," sighed the satisfied Rabbit to himself, "each precious pumpkin is a picture of perfection."

The sudden approach of an ominous buzzing caused Rabbit to look up, but there was no time for him to utter a word as Pooh, Piglet, Tigger, and Eeyore crashed past him, tumbling into the patch with the pumpkins, garden tools, and shreds of costume flying every which way!

The bees, seeing Rabbit standing stark still, swarmed at him in a humming hurricane of anger. At the very last instant, Rabbit realized his danger and ducked! The bees swooped over his head and between his ears, into the knothole of a tree behind him. The resourceful bunny quickly covered the hole with a bucket, trapping the belligerent bees inside.

However, before he had the time to even breathe a sigh of relief, Rabbit found himself face-to-face with a Pooh Bear who looked a great deal like Gopher in a red jersey with a pillow stuffed beneath it.

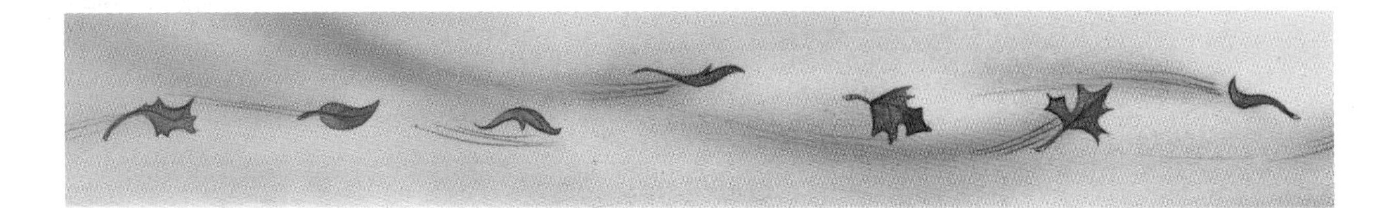

"Trick-or-treat," whistled Gopher-Pooh. And as if in response, the bees hammered the bucket aside and aimed straight for him!

"Oh, botherrrrrrrrr!" wailed Gopher-Pooh as he disappeared into the gathering gloom with the bees right behind him.

Rabbit surveyed the upheaval of his pumpkins and his friends and shook his head in exasperation.

"Of all my favorite holidays," he sighed forlornly, "Halloween *isn't*!"

Later, as Pooh, Piglet, Tigger, and Eeyore wandered woefully toward home in their ruined costumes, Tigger sadly observed his bedraggled outfit.

"This was the bestest skeletous costume of all time *ever*," he sniffled. Then he winked at Piglet. "An' I'm makin' no bones about it! Hoo-hoo-*hoo*!"

Very soon after, night fell and Halloween officially arrived. And arriving with it was a storm that chased wisps of clawlike clouds across the sky, playing hide-and-seek with the moon to the accompaniment of thundering rumbles.

Piglet scurried about his house, frantically blocking his door with furniture. And all about were posted very small signs that read, SPOOKABLES SCRAM! and NO GHOSTS ALLOWED! and GOBLINS GO HOME!

So, when a knock sounded on his front door, Piglet was not at all eager to answer it and dove beneath his favorite armchair.

"Who . . . who's there?" he squeaked, keeping his hands over his eyes.

"Why," responded a very Pooh-sounding voice, "it's me . . . them . . . *us*!"

"Pooh Bear?" said Piglet, peering out hopefully from under the armchair's dust ruffle. "How can I be certain it's truly really you? This could be a spookable trick!"

"Yes, I see, more or less," murmured Pooh from the other side of the door, where he stood with Tigger and Eeyore. "Though mostly less," he sighed.

"Perhaps if you say something only you could say," reasoned Piglet, "then I'd be certain it's you."

"What would that be?" asked the puzzled Pooh.

"How about 'I am Pooh'?" suggested Piglet.

"You are?" exclaimed the now totally confused bear of little brain. "Then who am I?"

"Pooh Bear!" squealed the delighted Piglet as he zipped out from under the chair, unblocked the door, and threw it open to reveal the smiling Pooh and Tigger and Eeyore.

NO GHOSTS ALLOWED
GOBLINS GO HOME

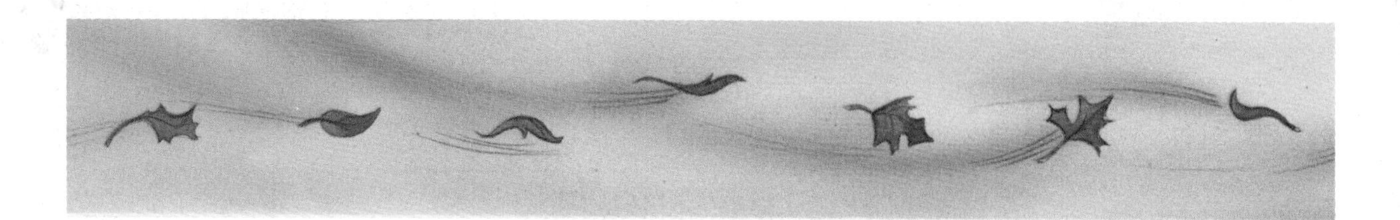

"Piglet," chuckled Pooh as he gave his best friend a hug. "You will be joining us for Halloween, won't you?"

Piglet looked at his friends guiltily and anxiously wrung his hands. "As a small and timid animal," he stammered nervously, "I'm afraid I'm really just *too* afraid." He hung his head sadly. "I'm very, *very* sorry, indeed."

"That's quite all right, Piglet," said Pooh Bear as he put a reassuring arm around his friend's very small shoulders. "We'll simply not have Halloween. This Halloween shall be a Hallo*wasn't*—and you shall have no reason to be afraid."

Piglet smiled up at Pooh gratefully. "Thank you, Pooh Bear," he said. "I think I shall be all right now."

Later that night, the storm began to rage fiercely through the Hundred-Acre Wood, twisting trees, rocking rocks, and howling horribly. Pooh watched it from his window and frowned.

"I hope Piglet is not too frightened," he sighed to himself. "He is, of course, all alone."

Pooh turned and thoughtfully gazed out of his window.

"I suspect something should be done." He frowned even more deeply. "But what?"

Scrunching his eyes together as tightly as they would go, Pooh concentrated fiercely. "Think-think-*think*!" he muttered. And, to no one's greater surprise than Pooh's, he did just that!

"Why," said Pooh when the thought hit him, "just because Piglet can't have Halloween with us, there's no reason we can't have Hallo*wasn't* with him!"

At Tigger's house, the fearless feline was putting the finishing touches

on a ghost costume. When he was done, he shook his head sadly.

"If only Piglet was more like me and less like him," he said to himself. "I'm not a-scared o'—"

At that moment Tigger's front door creaked open to reveal two sheet-shrouded figures on his doorstep.

"SPOOKABLES!" hollered Tigger, so frightened he tried to hide behind himself and tripped over his tail.

The "spookables" removed their sheets, and Pooh and Eeyore grinned down at the sprawled Tigger, who instantly bounced back to his feet.

"Pooh! Eeyore! Bet ya thought ya scared me, huh?" he exclaimed excitedly. "Well, ya did! Do it again, will ya? Pretty please?"

"We're on our way to Piglet's to have a Hallo*wasn't*," exclaimed Pooh. "Would you care to join us?"

Tigger snatched up his own ghost costume and charged out the door. "What're we standin' around here for?" he laughed.

At Piglet's house, the very small animal was pacing anxiously back and forth.

"Oh dear," he moped. "Everyone was so looking forward to Halloween." He sniffed and wiped away a very small tear from his eye. "I've let down Pooh and Tigger and Eeyore and Gopher . . . ," he exhaled a quivering sigh, ". . . and me!"

Pooh, Tigger, and Eeyore had almost reached Piglet's house through the fiercely blowing storm when a wayward tree branch snaked out and snagged a remnant of Pooh's bedsheet. In the wet and darkness, the bear was certain he'd been clutched by the cold claw of a spookable!

"Oh, my goodness!" shouted the startled Pooh. "Help! Spookables!"

Pooh's forlorn cry sounded over the racket kicked up by the storm.

"Pooh Bear?" Piglet gasped as he ran to his window.

Tigger and Eeyore, still wrapped in their ghostly bedsheets, were trying to free Pooh from the grasp of the uncooperative branch that had almost completely pulled the bear's costume off.

"Oh no!" Piglet cried at the sight of his best friend in a struggle with a pair of ghosts. "Spookables have Pooh!" A worried but determined expression came over his very small face. "I must save Pooh, Halloween or no Halloween!"

Suddenly noticing the remains of the pretend spookable scattered over the floor of his parlor, Piglet muttered under his breath, "I'll show those spookables what tricking and treating is all about!"

A few moments later, Piglet's front door was thrown open to reveal a spookable who looked very much like the one that had been constructed in Piglet's parlor.

"Boo?" said the spookable in a very small voice. Then, a bit louder, "I said, BOO!"

Pooh, Eeyore, and Tigger looked up in horror. "Spookable!" they wailed, and ran away down the path, leaving Pooh's torn costume in the possession of the grasping tree limb.

"Come back with my friend!" shouted the stilted spookable as it hobbled awkwardly down the hill after them.

Pooh, Tigger, and Eeyore ran past a startled Gopher, who was now clad in a Rabbit costume topped by long, floppy ears.

"Hey! What's the rush?" he snapped.

"Spookable!" wailed Pooh, Tigger, and Eeyore.

Gopher-Rabbit looked up the path just as the costumed Piglet lurched into him, and they both went rolling head over heels after the others!

Rabbit, trying to keep his pumpkins dry with a much-too-small umbrella, glanced up and had just enough time to mutter,

"Oh no! Not again!" Pooh, Tigger, and Eeyore collided with him. Then Piglet and Gopher collided with *them*, and everyone went rolling and sprawling through the pumpkins as pieces of costumes went flying every which way, and the rain fell, and the thunder rolled, and the lightning flashed!

A long moment passed.

Then they all carefully untangled themselves and discovered that there was not a single spookable to be seen, only the very wet and muddy friends and neighbors of the Hundred-Acre Wood.

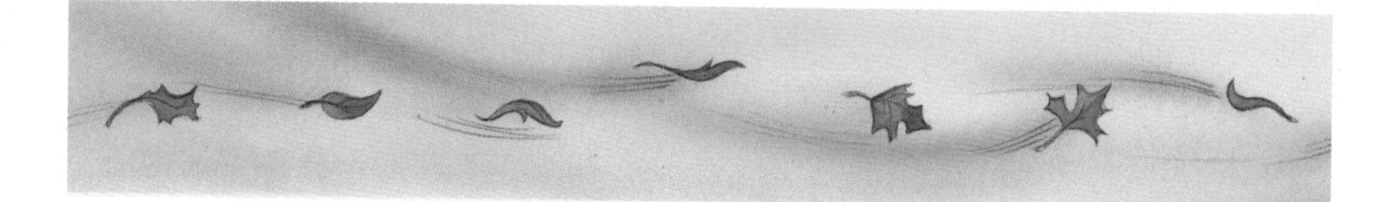

"Help!" squawked Gopher, making everyone jump. He was sitting in the midst of the garden with a hefty pumpkin on his shoulders and the oversize Rabbit ears, which were all that was left of his costume, poking out the top and waving in the breeze.

"What a wonderful costume, Gopher," said a very impressed Eeyore.

"It is?" responded the amazed Gopher.

"I particularly like the ears," agreed Rabbit.

"You do?" said Gopher.

"No doubt about it, Gopher," laughed Tigger, "it's the bestest costume yet!"

"Yippee!" cheered Gopher. "I knew I could do it!"

"And I knew Piglet could do it, too," announced Pooh as he helped his friend to his feet.

"Do what, Pooh Bear?" asked the puzzled Piglet.

"You saved us all," said Pooh.

"He did?" responded Tigger.

"Certainly!" explained Pooh. "He's here and the spookable isn't, so he must have chased it away."

Tigger looked about in wonder. "Say, that's right! Way to go, Piglet!"

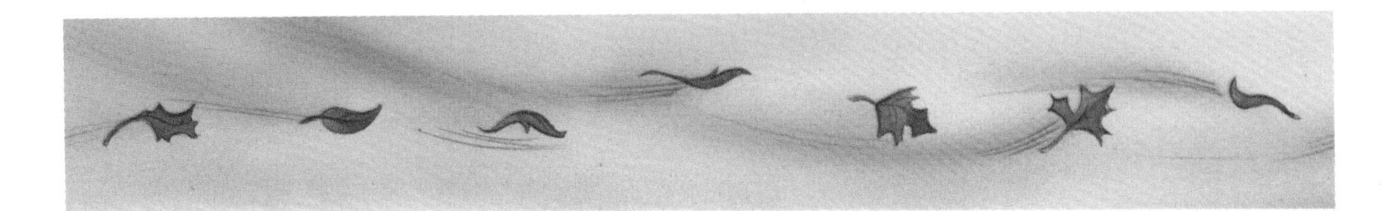

All Piglet's friends gathered around him and shook his very small hand as he puffed up with pride.

"Wait half a second, Piglet," said Tigger. "You never did figure out what you're gonna be for Halloween."

"Oh, but I have," smiled Piglet shyly. "I've decided to go as Pooh's very best and very bravest friend!"

"And *that*," said Pooh, smiling down at Piglet, "is the thing I'd most like you to be."